publisher: **ODDNESS**
artist: **MIKE DUBISCH**
editor: **CODY GOODFELLOW**

FORBIDDEN FUTURES 1 ISBN: 9781960213204 (V1.5)

THE PAST DEMANDS A REMATCH:

PASSION, PERSISTENCE & THE PULCHRITUDINOUS POWER OF PULP

by: CODY GOODFELLOW

WELCOME TO FORBIDDEN FUTURES!

The issue in your hands and those to come will bring you glimpses of the primordial, the penultimate and dreams outside time from the visionary mind of Mike Dubisch and many of the finest fantasists working today. Forthcoming issues will explore discrete themes and genres; but whether it's cosmic horror, retro-pulp futurism or comics, always the unspoken drive drawing it all together, is Mike's passion for the otherworldly, his uncanny ability to tap into some ineffable quality that feels like he's been spying on your dreams.

In a word, by love.

Love takes you to strange places, makes you do unthinkable things. It brought us together to bring you this thing you're reading, and we suspect you've come to us because you share this passion for the otherworldly and half-remembered fantasies in cold hard print.

When I first came across the art of Mike Dubisch in his Morbid Curiosity collection, it was hidden among a shambles of indie and underground commix and graphic novels in a dusty corner of a Santa Monica comic shop. With that one book, Mike resoundingly introduced himself and reminded me why I love monsters, and why I haunt these bins and long-boxes.

Every horror comic fan knows that to the suspension of disbelief must be added the suspension of disappointment, the burden of keeping the guttering love and anticipation alive through an ever-deepening blizzard of crap neutered by comics codes, derivative storytelling or just lousy technique; but buried among mountains of flaky disappointment, here was the real gold. The arc of his fusion of so many beloved influences into a coherent and uniquely mutated style compelled me keep it close by my desk as the kind of brain-fuel I thrive on when writing.

Later that year, when cruising the labyrinthine dealer's floor of San Diego Comic-Con, by happy accident, I encountered Mike in the flesh, doing sketches at a booth. I found him to be not only humble and lovable, but driven by the same obsessions with monsters and horror comics as I, and hungry to create stuff that would not only repay those hallowed childhood influences, but push them forward.

Strange places.

Unthinkable things.

Sure, this chain of circumstance might still have gone down similarly in a purely digital world, but the purity of print and its inimitable tendency to find its way into your life when it's needed most, is a gift to which we all feel profoundly indebted. All the accidental encounters with a friend or stranger's comic collection, all the forgotten gems among the jetsam in used bookshops and thrift store and library sale bins, came to seem like destiny, like the patient, serendipitous seduction by wizards from a weird realm just behind batwing doors in the back of every comic shop.

If this is a generational condition, then it will die with us, or mutate into something else. Happy digital accidents persist, and a vast sampling of fantastic sequential and genre art can still be discovered, but the Internet cannot tell you what it has forgotten, doesn't care much for anything not currently for sale.

Love of print is hardly a generational thing, but the end of it will be. Print sales of books and single-issue comics continue to outpace digital, despite price hikes and other market-shrinking factors, but mainstream publishers have a stake in killing print exclusive of economic concerns as part of the corporate move to deny you ownership of the media you buy and even solid consumer products, replacing it with a license like the software terms agreements we never read. Print belongs to you in a way digital simply can't, and that intimacy only deepens, becomes an intimate collaboration between artist, author and reader.

Comics as a medium might well have slid into the arcane hobbyists' netherworld of numismatists and philatelists, if superhero comics hadn't spawned the most valuable intellectual property in our culture and become wholly synonymous with the medium itself. A weird paradox for readers like myself, who only came to superhero comics for the monsters, and those monsters who sometimes fight crime with their underwear outside their pants.

Always a beloved but marginal presence, horror comics as a genre has been as much a victim of its success as their failures. Ankled by the comics code from depicting anything remotely horrific, mainstream horror comics cleaved to a watered-down version of the morality-play anthology formula of the EC comics, with one foot firmly planted in a real world better portrayed in cinema, long after the code became irrelevant. Warren's Creepy and Eerie kept horror for the love of horror alive with far-out art bolstering often hackneyed or half-baked scripts, but still observed stern decency standards to stay on newsstands. Eerie, more importantly, broke out of the anthology format with a stable of recurring characters in serialized stories, demonstrating the kind of deeper, weirder stories you could only get at with a monster as your hero. Only through sporadic and uneven underground work like Last Gasp, Pacific and other indies, and Heavy Metal and hard-to-find European imports, could one find genre art with the curb-feelers and training wheels cut off.

But even with the horror boom following the monster-positive success of Hellboy, too many modern horror comics feel like storyboards for high concept movies. Even Hellboy only went to Hell after his many Gothic pulp adventures ran together into a homogeneous mush, and a long, introspective hiatus.

Granted, no comics project reaches fruition without someone sweating blood for it, but all too often, the element of the impossible enters into a world too much like our own, or grafted onto another genre. Cowboy… zombies… pirate… vampires… Devil… gangsters… reshuffle until optioned. Far too few fantasy and horror comics start in the weird place, and then go digging into what's under it, and nobody goes in there with more tangible zeal than Dubisch.

Alongside his many other virtues, Mike is a fearless creator. With Weirdling, he confidently hatched a deeply bizarre reality that was only the outer layer of a Dante's Inferno of cosmic surrealism. With Crypt Kid, he conjures a family-friendly (for older, weirder kids, anyway) young ghoul as our reliable guide to an underworld uniquely his own.

Naturally, we hope this issue of Forbidden Futures will be the first of many. But even if this is also the last one, we hope to share with you the love of holding the unimaginable in your hands, and that by setting it adrift in print, Crypt Kid and countless other creations will continue to spread the love of strange places and unthinkable things long after the lights have gone out and the Internet is just another story the tribal shaman tells.

SKINNY MINNIE

JOHN SKIPP

YOU'D THINK SHE'D BE FATTER, GIVEN HOW MUCH SHE FUCKING EATS, CHAINED TO THE TABLE, DOING ALMOST NOTHING BUT.

But when what's left of Don's head lands on the plate before her, with his lushly-crested pate already lopped off at mid-forehead, Skinny Minnie digs right in. It's like cranium soufflé, or brains tartar. Were she capable of happiness, I would say this is it. Every morsel an unparalleled treat.

The drugs don't seem to be hurting, either, at least in terms of keeping her focused. A little injection goes a long, long way.

And she has a long, long way to go.

Never thought of myself as a big-on-revenge guy. That always seemed like a lower emotion. But now that I know just how low we can go, it seems downright borderline uplifting. Like there couldn't be a better fucking use of my time, here in our last days left.

The attic of Don's never-too-occupied skull empties out quickly in her two-clawed assault, Minnie licking her fingers when the bowl is empty, then ripping away at the plump, juicy cheeks. I hope she remembers not to pop those peepers, though the bowl we're reserving for her desert is overflowing already. So many mocking eyes to meet.

You never think of how many people have hurt you until you line them all up and kill them, one by one.

And you never feel like justice has been done until the one who wronged you wrongest has to sin-eat them all. And love it.

Oh, Skinny Minnie. You're a much better zombie than you ever were a human.

Eat up, baby. Eat up

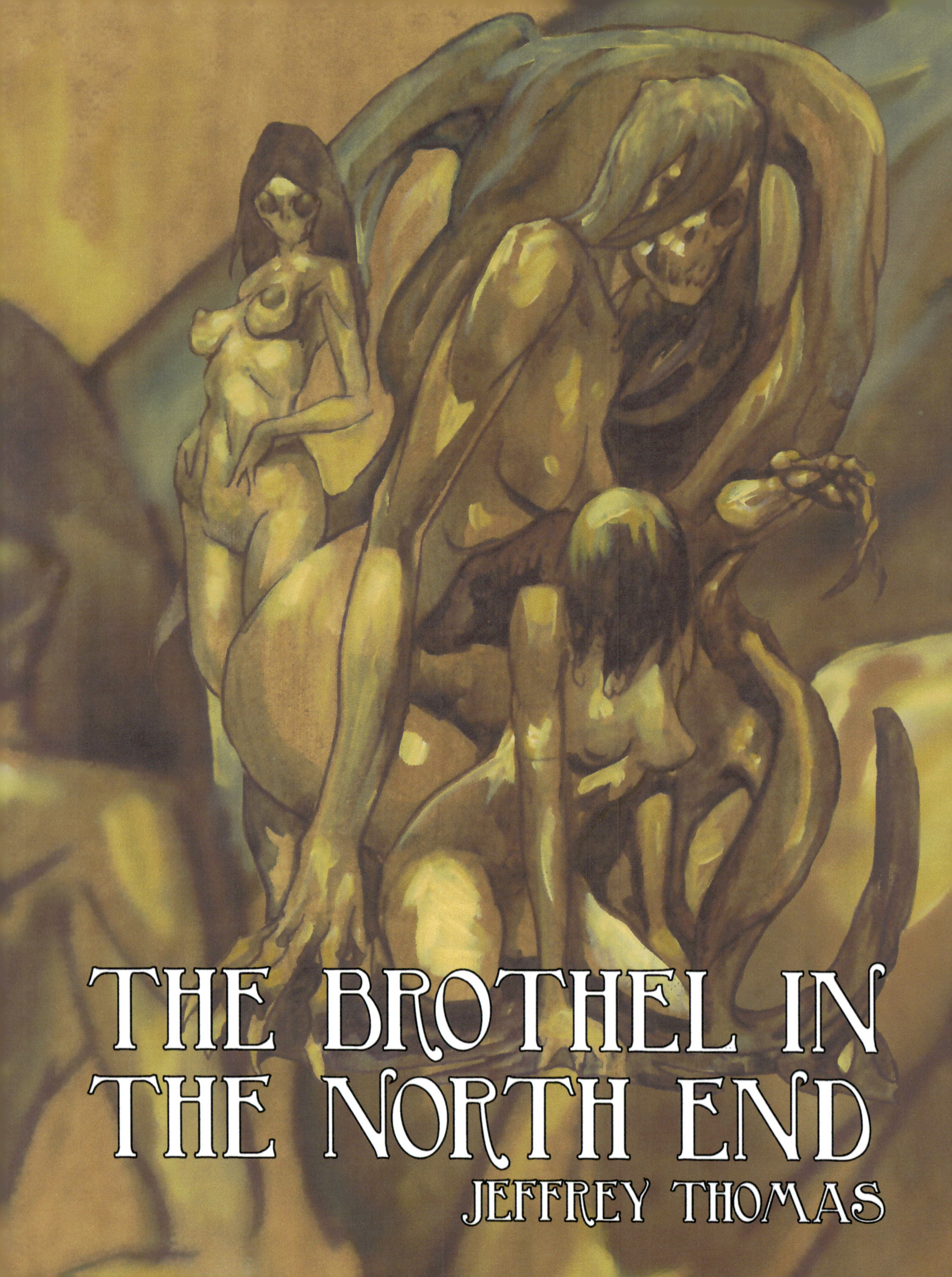

THE BROTHEL IN
THE NORTH END
JEFFREY THOMAS

T HE HOUSE, BUILT IN 1910 BUT NOWADAYS CALLED A CONDO, was on Hull Street in Boston's North End... a nondescript row house fused with a line of such units, forming a quaint wall of red brick. The street was so narrow that cars could only pass along it in one direction. Across the street from this wall of brick condos, and the row of cars parked tightly in front of them, was the Copp's Hill Burying Ground.

On the other side of the ancient cemetery, on Charter Street, was the domicile of the controversial artist Enoch Coffin. The owner of the house on Hull Street, aware of Coffin's interest in painting extraordinary subject matter, once invited Coffin to visit and paint whatever he saw that captured his fancy. Coffin was promised he would discover a wealth of inspiration for his grotesque work. However, upon realizing what went on at that address, the artist turned down the request of his company.

The owner of the house on Hull Street, a man named William Aiken, was insulted by this rejection. Being permitted entrance to his home was an honor that his guests paid great sums for. But then, Aiken supposed Coffin was jaded. His guests had never seen anything like what he had to offer behind that unremarkable and inscrutable door of his.

A stone-lined tunnel ran beneath Hull Street, under the line of expensive parked cars, unbeknownst to Aiken's neighbors in the condos wedged cheek to jowl against his own. This cramped tunnel communicated between Aiken's basement and an ant-like series of earthen tunnels beneath the cemetery. He kept the door to that tunnel tightly locked on his side, however, only unbolting it when he had hired men with him. Hired men with guns. And he only unbolted it when it was time to summon the females.

It was in his basement that he had created his brothel.

Oh, Aiken's guests were jaded, too, in their own way. Money had bought them women of every race and shape and age. Children, both female and male. Money had permitted some of his customers the luxury of snuffing the life from their fleshly toys. But even the most jaded of them had never, before coming to the house on Hull Street, lain with a being that was not human.

These bestial subterranean beings, white as albino cave animals, were encrusted with dirt, with blood from the dogs and homeless people they fed upon, encrusted with the decay of the long-dead corpses they crunched their semi- canine jaws into, encrusted with mold and their sweat. They stank, and that was part of their appeal for Aiken's wealthy patrons, who lived their lives among people with showered, perfumed, neatly attired bodies that belied their inner filth.

The females would be lured from the tunnel, fitted with muzzles and bound with restraints at wrist and ankle to prevent them from giving in to their nature in the throes of passion, but they were not forced to engage in these sexual acts. In payment for their acquiescence, before they were tied down they attacked and feasted upon the sacrifices the brothel customers had brought with them: human escorts, who had been led down into Aiken's soundproofed basement, unaware of what their johns truly had in mind for them.

After they had been sated, the lean and carnal female ghouls—their naked white breasts slathered in blood, their sharp-boned faces masked in gore, shreds of flesh crammed between the ragged teeth hidden behind their muzzles–willingly laid down on the three hospital beds Aiken had arranged in his basement. He only ever accepted up to three customers into his brothel at any one time. Only up to three ghouls were permitted through the door. Aiken didn't want to worry about too many escorts being reported missing at any one time. More importantly, he didn't want his hired men to have to watch over more than three ghouls at any one time. There was always the threat that their sacrifices would not be enough to satisfy them, once their bloodlust was stoked.

Aiken took precautions against the ghouls, but ultimately he didn't take sufficient precautions against his hired men. One night one of them, feeling he hadn't been paid adequately for his services, and had been verbally abused by his employer, sneaked back into the basement alone before he left the residence on Hull Street, and unbolted that door to the tunnel under the street.

Despite their arrangement, the ghouls couldn't resist their nature any longer...it was too long between the sacrifices Aiken offered them. And the males had grown jealous of the meals their females were offered.

The next time Aiken ventured alone into his basement, he became the last of the sacrifices in the brothel in the North End.

DIABOLICUS INTERRUPTUS

Christine Morgan

THE PENETRATION, HARD AND FAST, SINKING DEEP.

A cry, part pain, part pleasure.

The hot, thick gush of spurting wetness.

Bodies writhing, skin slick, her breath hot and her touch hotter … his flesh is still cool, but warming now, warming and flushing from her blood as he drinks and drinks … her blood filling his veins, suffusing his tissues … and when she feels him stiffen against her, the knowledge that it is her own blood somehow adds to her passion, her arousal.

She grasps that stiffness, his cock so much larger than his fangs, and guides it to the hungry cleft between her thighs. Moist and open, she welcomes this other penetration, this filling thrust and plunge. Her spine arches, her wings flare wide, her tail curls and lashes.

And he, the vampire of her two lovers, rears back his head, ripping his teeth from her neck, as he voices his own infernal lust. A mouthful of blood spills down her body, coursing the contours, a red river over her tits. She seizes him, dragging his mouth down again, wanting it all, cock and fangs driving to the hilt. Her nails, her claws, blacker than midnight and needle-sharp, rake at him to release yet more stolen demonic blood. He bites, he thrusts, and her hellcunt clasps and squeezes.

Wanting more, more and yet more, craving more, she coils her tail around the hairless green form at her feet. This second lover, this goblin-ghoul, has been doing some biting of his own.

A feasting bite, a ravenous gnawing and chewing, savoring the soft meat of her calves. His tongue slathers the wounds, his saliva tingles and stings and heightens her every sensation.

With that coiled tail, she urges him upward, and he needs no further encouragement before he is kneeling behind her, eagerly burying his face in her ass. Even as the vampire continues his fucking and sucking, the goblin-ghoul feasts upon ripe, rounded buttocks. His long tongue worms into her, delving, squirming further up the passage of her nethers than humanly possible.

Not that humanly possible matters much here. The demoness and her lovers twist and contort, entwining in unimaginable positions, each climax building toward some unspeakable, apocalyptic conclusion.

But, in the moments before that conclusion can be reached, the chamber in which their unholy orgy takes place undergoes a violent jolt, knocking them asunder. The ceiling splits. In floods a beam of terrible light, celestial in its clarity and devastating in its glare. A figure descends through this harshly brilliant rift, a figure with majestic white wings and shining god–armor, a sword like forged lightning gripped in one hand.

The lovers flinch, shielding their eyes. The gouges and scratches on their bodies are starkly revealed, nipples bitten off, genitals claw-shredded, blood and semen and other fluids streaking their skin.

"So," bellows the angel in a voice of thunder. "Here is where I find you, Adoriel!"

The demoness cowers, attempting to cover her despoiled nudity. Her aspect slips briefly, voluptuous curves melting into androgyny, the leathery folds of batlike wings transforming to shining seraphic plumage. The others, the vampire and the goblin-ghoul, gape at her in astonishment.

"Slumming in the sin-pits of Hell!" the angel's thunderous condemnation continues. "Indulging your foulest carnal urges, fornicating—"

Just then, the chamber jolts again, and again

… the ceiling splitting a second time, and a third. More light pours in, pure, unbearable. These fornicators in the sin-pits of Hell cringe and cower as more angels descend, glorious in their armor, wreathed in coronas of light.

"Well, well, well," the first angel tells the demoness—whose true nature is now becoming more revealed—in a more conversational, almost cruelly amused tone, "You must have really pissed Him off—"

"So!" shouts the second angel, as unto a thousand trumpets of judgment and doom. "This is where—"

"So!" roars the third, a lion of fire, a dragon of righteous wrath. "This—"

Beholding each other, they pause in confusion, then set to arguing.

"I was sent to—"

"No, I was!"

And they, two angels, face off with weapons raised, as if they might strike at each other.

"Stop!" The first angel steps between them, arms and wings outstretched. "Whatever the cause of this misunderstanding, let us solve it back home. We have found Adoriel; that is what matters."

"Adoriel?" they echo, a baffled chorus.

One adds, pointing fiery sword at the cringing vampire, "I am here for Tatheal."

"But I," says the other in almost the same breath, indicating the goblin-ghoul, "came in search of Samchiel."

Silence holds for its own stretching eternity, a stunned silence during which all demonic and monstrous guises fall away. The demoness, vampire, and goblin-ghoul stand revealed in their own true forms, nude and sexless. Their shoulders slump, their wings droop. They hang their heads and avert their gazes.

It is indeed going to be an awkward return to Heaven.

WHAT'RE YOU LOOKIN' AT, CITY-BOY? WE STOOKEYS ARE PROUD, GOD-FEARIN' FOLK. CLAN LAW SAYS WE SHALL NOT WEAR FANCY MIXED FIBER CLOTHES OR UNCLEAN ANIMAL HIDES. NO SIR, UNTIL A STOOKEY BOY IS READY TO CLAIM MANHOOD, HE GOES FORTH NAKED AS ADAM.

THE SKIN OFF YOUR BACK

TRACTOR PULL!!

WHEN HE'S READY TO GO INTO TOWN OR JUST COURT OUTSIDE HIS OWN HOUSEHOLD, ALL A YOUNG STOOKEY BUCK HAS TO DO IS PICK A FIGHT AT THE FULL-MOON HOOTENANNY AND CHALLENGE A SOFTER-SKINNED COUSIN TO A GOOD OL' FASHIONED TRACTOR PULL.

AIN'T MUCH TO THE RULES. PULLS SOMETIMES GO FOR HOURS, IF BOTH BOYS ARE REAL LEATHERNECKS.

AIN'T MUCH TO WIN, EITHER, BUT IF YOU DO, YOU GET A NEW SUIT OF PROPER CLOTHES. (MY DADDY, HE GOT ENOUGH TO MAKE A FINE PAIR OF OVERALLS OFF HIS BROTHER, BUT HE DIDN'T CARE FOR IT AND GANGRENE GOT HIM.)

BUT ONCE YOU WIN, YOU CAN'T NEVER TAKE IT OFF—NOT TO SWIM, NOT TO SLEEP, NOR EVEN TO BREED, LEST THE LOSER COME BACK FOR A REMATCH. SO I SAY AGAIN... WHAT'RE YOU LOOKIN' AT?!

MIKE DUBISCH
THE CRYPT KID

AN AGE BEYOND THE DAY THAT
DEMONS AND MONSTERS
FROM BENEATH ROSE UP TO
CLAIM THE SURFACE OF THE EARTH.

A WORLD WHERE
HUMAN BEINGS ARE NOW SCARCE,
AND EVEN THESE DRINKERS
OF HUMAN BLOOD AND THESE EATERS
OF HUMAN FLESH GO HUNGRY.

EVEN THE LOWLIEST OF THE INVADERS,
THE CARRION EATER, THE GHOULS,
FIGHT OVER DESICCATED SCRAPS.

RAAAARR!
SOMETHING APPROACHES!
HISSS!
CLEAR OUT, TRASH! THERE'S A HUMAN HERE. WE SHALL NOT SHARE OUR FIRST MEAT IN MONTHS WITH THE LIKES OF YOU.

IT'S CLOSE.
PREPARE TO
FEED, MY
FRIEND!

DUST!

HELLO?
AH...
THERE YOU ARE. HELLO.
IT'S OK. I WON'T GET TOO CLOSE.
YOU WON'T HURT ME, WILL YOU?
HERE... I UNDERSTAND YOUR KIND CAN TAKE SUSTENANCE FROM OUR BLOOD.

DON'T
WORRY.

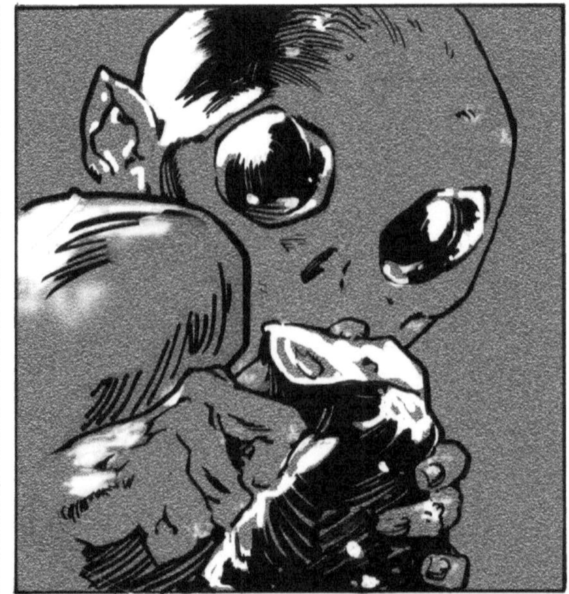

IT'S COLD.

WAIT!
DON'T GO—
I NEED...
I *NEED*
TO *TALK*
TO YOU...

INCREDIBLE.
IT'S TRUE.

YOUR KIND HAS POWER WHEN YOU CONSUME COLD REMAINS.
SINCE MY FLESH IS WARM...
I NEED NOT FEAR YOU...

I HAVE MORE FOR YOU— BUT... I NEED YOUR HELP.
I HAVE BEEN LOOKING FOR ONE OF YOUR KIND.
FOR ONE SUCH AS YOU.

FOOD, AND SOMETIMES... CARRIERS OF YOUR- *SUPERNATURAL AFFLICTIONS.*
WE HUMANS- FOR YOUR KIND, YOU *SUPERNATURALS*... WE ARE NOTHING BUT *FOOD.*

SO MANY LOST TO THE VIRUS THAT MAKES *VAMPIRES* OF US.
OTHERS TO THEIR UNQUENCHABLE *THIRST.*
SOME HAVE SURVIVED BY BECOMING SLAVES OR THRALLS.

OUR HISTORY IS OVER.
BUT MANY OF US HAVE HIDDEN AND TRIED TO DISCOVER HOW TO FIGHT...
BUT INSTEAD, WE FOUND SOMETHING ELSE.
WE DISCOVERED... THE SUPERNATURALS!
YOU'RE JUST THE FIRST WAVE. *SOMETHING ELSE IS COMING-*
SOMETHING WORSE- DARKER... *HUNGRIER.*

I DON'T KNOW IF THIS WORLD IS WORTH SAVING ANYMORE.
BUT IN THIS BAG, I HAVE A WEAPON. I CAN'T MAKE THE JOURNEY ON MY OWN. NO HUMAN COULD... BUT WITH YOUR HELP...
IF I CAN GIVE YOU MORE OF THOSE, WILL YOU HELP ME? WHEN IT'S DONE, I'LL BRING YOU WHERE OUR DEAD ARE STILL.. FLESH. NOT DUST... WHAT DO YOU SAY?
HER NAME IS KAREN. SHE HAS KNOWLEDGE OF AN ENTRANCE TO THE UNDERGROUND.
YOUNG... THOUGH SHE IS A VETERAN SOLDIER OF THIS HELL-SCAPE. THE SMALL GHOUL ALSO IS PRACTICED AT THE CRAFT OF SURVIVAL. THEY DESCEND QUICKLY, GUIDED BY INSTINCT, A ROUGH PLAN OF THE CAVERNS, AND THE THIN BEAM OF HER TORCH.

WAIT-
I THINK I HEARD SOMETHING...
BLAM BLAM BLAM

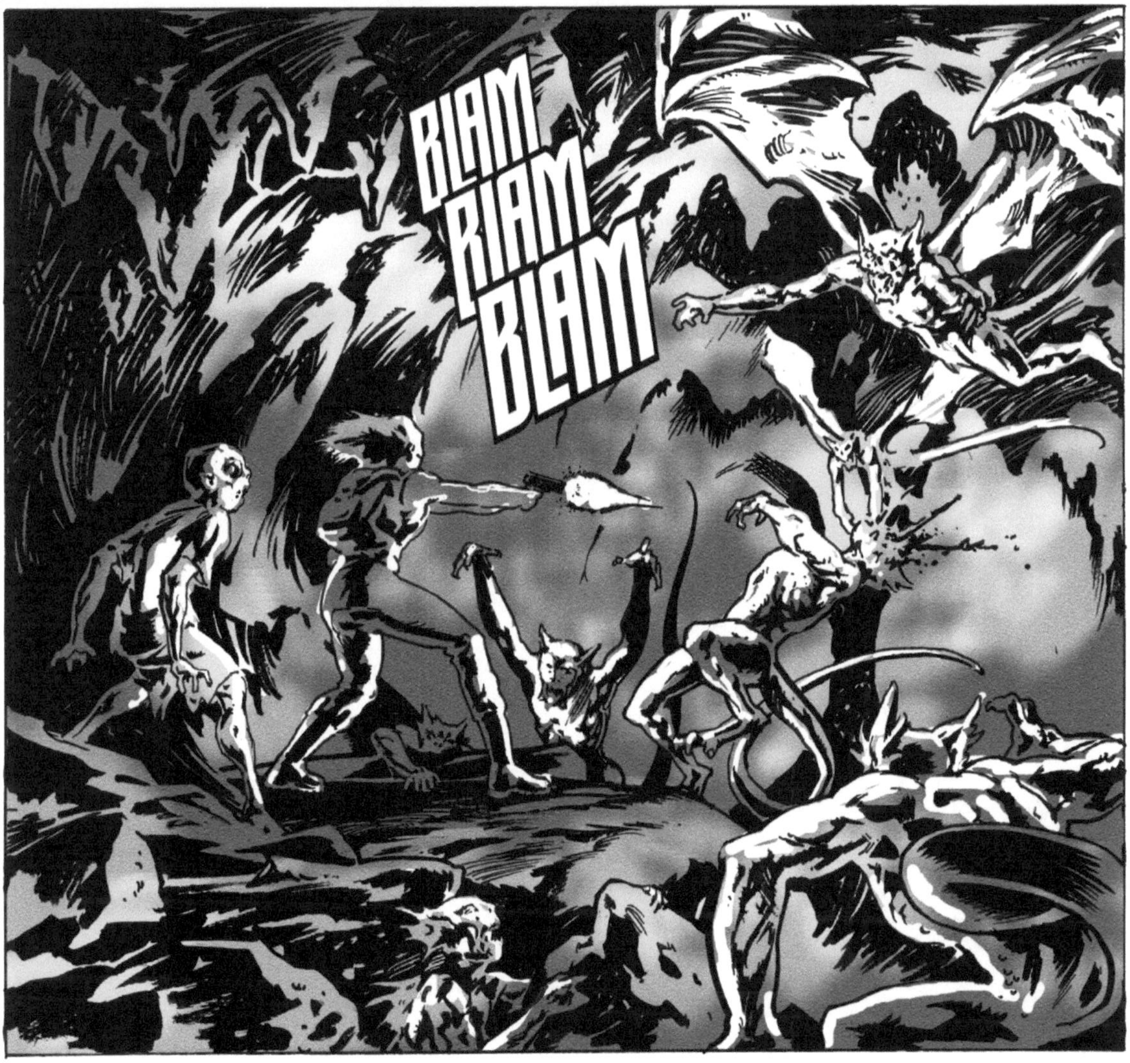

THE GIRL'S KEEN AIM AND LOADED WEAPON MAKE THEM TOUGHER PREY THAN THE SUBTERRANEANS EXPECT, AND THEY WITHDRAW WITH A FEW LESS MOUTHS TO FEED.
THEY'LL BE BACK. *THEM* OR *OTHERS*. WE'RE BEING *TRACKED*.

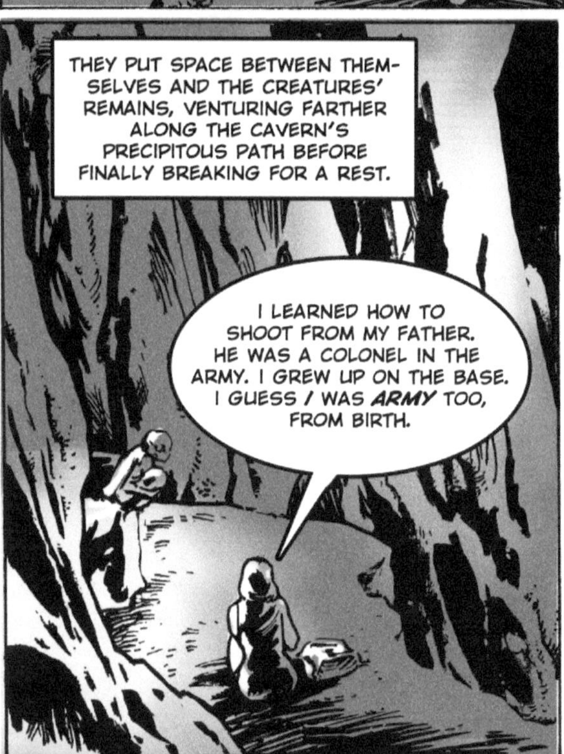

THEY PUT SPACE BETWEEN THEM- SELVES AND THE CREATURES' REMAINS, VENTURING FARTHER ALONG THE CAVERN'S PRECIPITOUS PATH BEFORE FINALLY BREAKING FOR A REST.
I LEARNED HOW TO SHOOT FROM MY FATHER. HE WAS A COLONEL IN THE ARMY. I GREW UP ON THE BASE. I GUESS *I* WAS *ARMY* TOO, FROM BIRTH.

DIDN'T SEE MUCH OF *MOM*. SHE LIVED OFF THE BASE. THEY WEREN'T TOGETHER, MY PARENTS.
PARENTS?

YEAH, PARENTS- MOM, DAD... DON'T YOU HAVE PARENTS? AREN'T YOU... *BORN*?
WE COME OUT OF DARKNESS. OUT FROM THE EARTH.
AND *THAT* IS ALL *WE* KNOW OF THE ORIGINS OF YOUR KIND AS WELL.
SOME BELIEVE IT. IT MIGHT EXPLAIN YOUR NEED TO FEED ON FLESH THAT ONCE HELD A *HUMAN SOUL*.

BUT ME, I DON'T THINK SO..
"I DON'T BELIEVE IT," SHE SAYS. "YOU HAD TO HAVE BEEN BORN. YOU HAVE TO HAVE PARENTS, SOMEWHERE, EVEN IF YOU DON'T REMEMBER THEM."
THE SMALL GHOUL SEARCHES FOR A MEMORY OF A NURTURING FIGURE AND SEES ONLY THE GIRL IN FRONT OF HIM.
NO LONGER REPELLED BY HER BODY HEAT- HE FEELS DRAWN TO HER. SHE IS A PROTECTOR, A PROVIDER.
IT NO LONGER EVEN SEEMS ODD FOR HIM TO TAKE FOOD RIGHT FROM HER HANDS.
BURNING WITH THE POWER OF THE FEEDING, THE SMALL GHOUL FINDS HE CAN BE A POWERFUL PARTNER AGAINST THE ENEMY WHO STALKED THEM.

RIAM
BLAM
WITH REPEATED FEEDINGS, THE GHOUL'S STRENGTH GROWS- THE HUNGER IN THE BELLIES OF THEIR ATTACKERS MAKES THEM DESPERATE- BUT ALSO WEAKER, AND AGAIN AND AGAIN, THEY ARE CHASED OFF, DEFEATED, OR SLAIN.

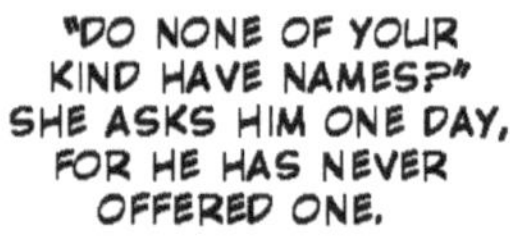
"DO NONE OF YOUR KIND HAVE NAMES?" SHE ASKS HIM ONE DAY, FOR HE HAS NEVER OFFERED ONE.

I DON'T KNOW.
PERHAPS...

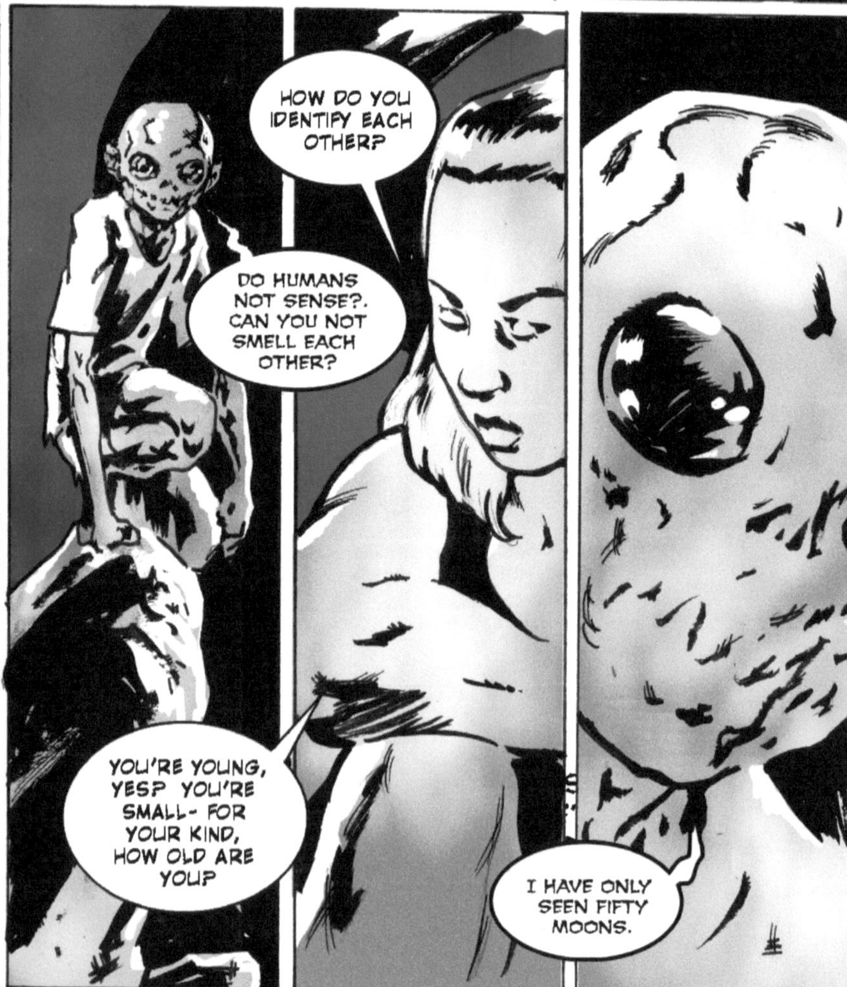
HOW DO YOU IDENTIFY EACH OTHER?
DO HUMANS NOT SENSE?. CAN YOU NOT SMELL EACH OTHER?
YOU'RE YOUNG, YES? YOU'RE SMALL- FOR YOUR KIND, HOW OLD ARE YOU?
I HAVE ONLY SEEN FIFTY MOONS.

YOU'RE ONLY FOUR YEARS OLD. YOU'RE JUST A KID.

WATCH YOUR STEP H...

WHOA-!

HELP!! PULL ME UP!!

GRAB MY HAND!!

PLEASE TAKE MY HAND.

THANKS, KID.

FORBIDDEN FUTURES

THE MOMENT IS NOT LOST ON EITHER OF THEM; HAD HE ALLOWED HER TO FALL, THE GHOUL COULD HAVE HAD THE REMAINING PACKETS FROM HER SACK AND PERHAPS FEASTED ON HER FLESH AS WELL...
I'VE TASTED IT TOO. HUMAN...MEAT. WE WERE HOLED UP- BESIEGED, BY VAMPIRES.
WE HAD DEAD, COMPANIONS.... EVEN FRIENDS, WHO HAD FALLEN- THEY WERE IN COLD STORAGE...

THERE ISN'T MUCH A PERSON WON'T DO TO SURVIVE.
I DOUBT THERE ARE MANY WHO HAVEN'T HAD TO DO WHAT WE DID.
IT DOESN'T MAKE YOU EVIL...
JUST A SURVIVOR.

KAREN!
KID!

HANG ON, KID!

BLAM
RIAM
BLAM

KILL HER MY BROTHERS! TONIGHT WE FEAST!

BLAM
RIAM
BLBIAM
RIAM
BLAM
HER LITTLE FRIEND CAN GNAW ON HER BONES!

BLAM

GO GET 'EM, KID.

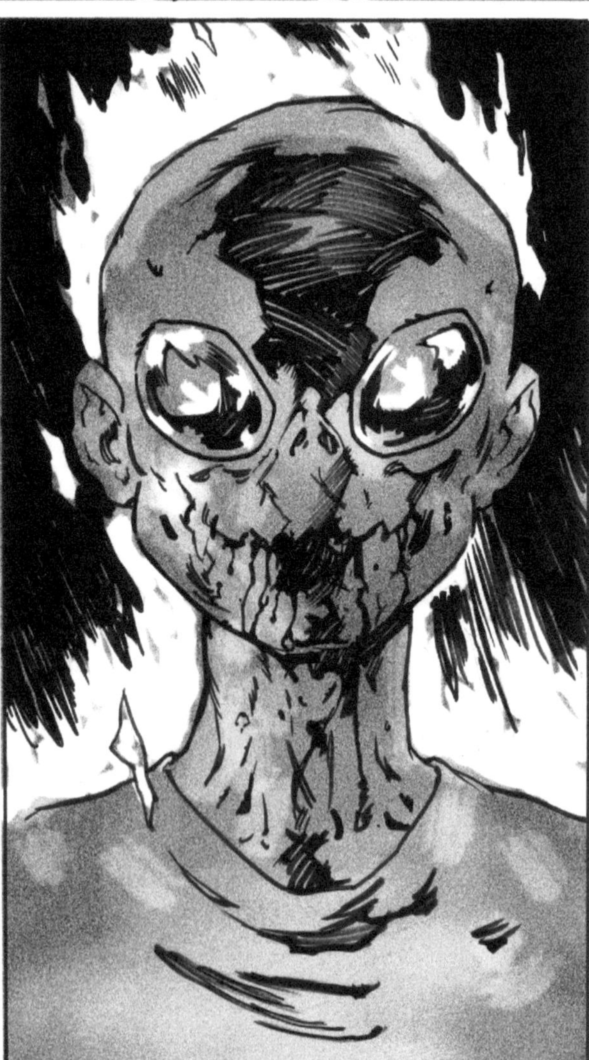

FOR SOME TIME, THE CAVES HAVE BEEN GETTING WARMER. NOW, AS THE TWO DESCEND, THE WALLS LUMINESCE- THEY ARE ENTERING THE ABANDONED HEART OF THE SUPERNATURALS' SUBTERRANIAN WORLD....
IT'S THE CREEPING THREAT, THE THING FROM BELOW.

THERE IT IS. IT'S MILES AWAY, STILL...
THE SMALL GHOUL'S EYES NEED NO ASSISTANCE.
YES, I SEE IT...

THROUGH A CRACK IN THE FLOOR OF THE CHASM, IT THROBS ITS DARK HUNGER. THE GHOUL FEELS ITS DEEP PULSATION THROUGH MILES OF STONE IN HIS BONES AND FLESH.

THESE RUINS... DEMONS DWELLED HERE.

THEY'VE ALL MOVED OUT...

WHATS MOVED IN?

WAIT... WHAT HAVE WE WANDERED *INTO?*

ARE THOSE...

UH-OH.

HISSS!!

ONCE, THIS CITY HOUSED A GREAT UNDERGROUND PEOPLE. THEN DEMONS AND VAMPIRES TOOK UP RESIDENCE IN ITS RUINS.

NOW, INSECTS FROM THE DEPTHS HAVE EXTENDED THEIR SCOURGE UP INTO THIS PLACE.

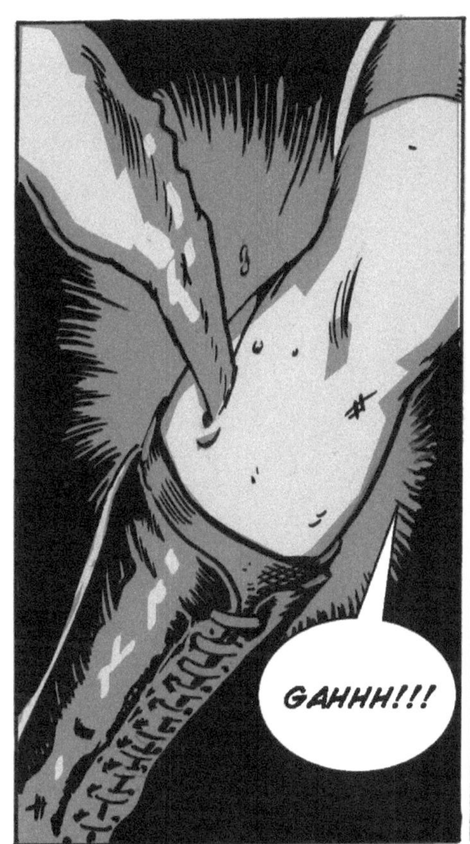

GAHHH!!!

FOOD IS SCARCE FOR ALL IN THIS TWILIGHT OF EARTH; THE INSECTS MOVED QUICKLY ON THEIR PREY.
KID! MY LEG... IT'S NUMB.

BLAM
BLAM

KID!!!
GET US OUT OF HERE!

COME, HOLD ON TO ME, KAREN..

THE SMALL GHOUL FINALLY EVADES THE RAVENOUS GRUBS.

THEY STOP TO REST AND ASSESS THE DAMAGE FROM THE INSECT'S TALON...
I DON'T KNOW, KID....
I'LL BE ABLE TO WALK ON IT, BUT...

"I MAY BE A BIT-
UNSTEADY!"

THE YOUNG GHOUL
VOWS TO STAY
CLOSE...

BUT THE PATHWAY
DOWNWARD
CONTINUES TO BE
UNRELIABLE...

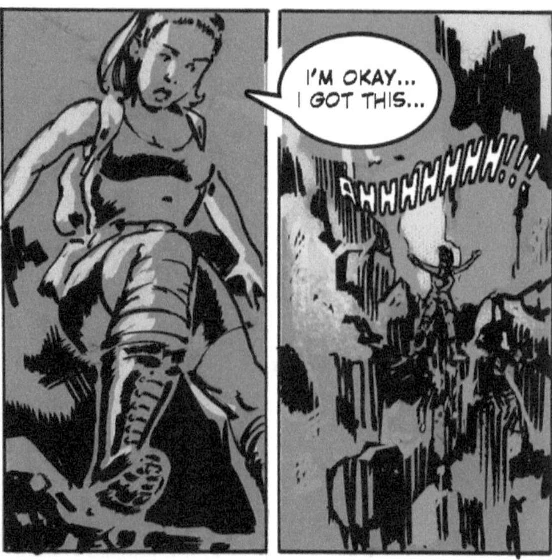
I'M OKAY...
I GOT THIS...

AHHHHHHHH!!!

SHE FALLS IN A
HAIL OF DEBRIS...

AND LANDS WITH
A SICKENING CRUNCH.

KAREN!

KID! HELP...
HELP ME REACH MY BAG...

I'M A GONER... I CAN'T MOVE...

THE WEAPON?
KID...

YOU NEED... TO KNOW...

IT'S POISON— ONE THAT WOULD HAVE *TAKEN* MY LIFE...
THEN RAPIDLY COOLED MY FLESH.
YOU WERE TO PARTAKE OF MY FLESH, WE'D HOPED...
THEN USE YOUR POWER TO BATTLE THE THING OF DARKNESS...

YOU, KID... YOU ARE THE WEAPON.

BUT *I BLEW* IT.
I'M GOING TO DIE, NOW...

YOU'LL FEED HERE, IN THIS FORGOTTEN, USELESS CAVERN.
NOW ALL IS LOST...

STILL WARM…

FINALLY, HE IS IN THE REALM OF THE THING OF DARKNESS, THE CREEPING EVIL.

IT'S AWAKE. ITS ROAR IS IN THE GHOUL'S EARS.

IT'S COMING. FROM THE DEPTHS OF HELL, IT RISES.

IT IS STILL SEVERAL DAYS JOURNEY, BUT THE BLOOD BAGS ARE GONE.
THE GIRL'S BODY SHOWS SIGNS OF DECAY. THE SMELL SHOULD BE IRRESISTIBLE TO THE GHOUL.

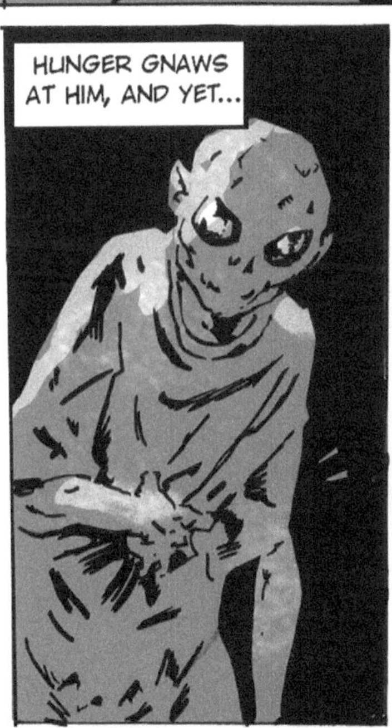
HUNGER GNAWS AT HIM, AND YET...

STILL TOO WARM...

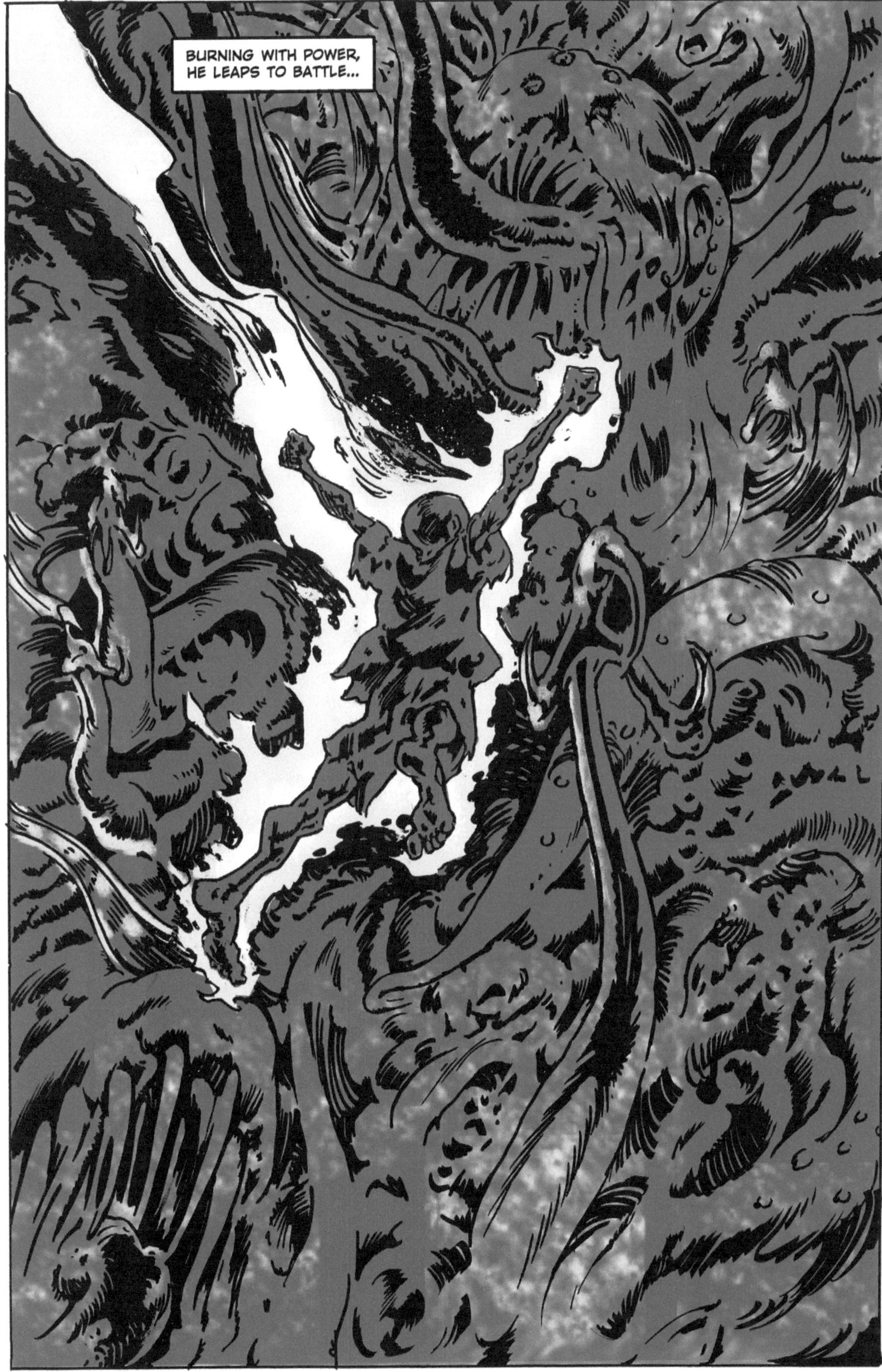
BURNING WITH POWER,
HE LEAPS TO BATTLE...

PLUNGING INTO
THE HEART
OF CHAOS
AND EVIL....

QUESTING FOR THE VORTEX OF DARKNESS, THE PULSING EPICENTER OF MALEVOLENCE...

AND SUDDENLY
NOT ALONE.

I'M HERE
WITH YOU,
KID...

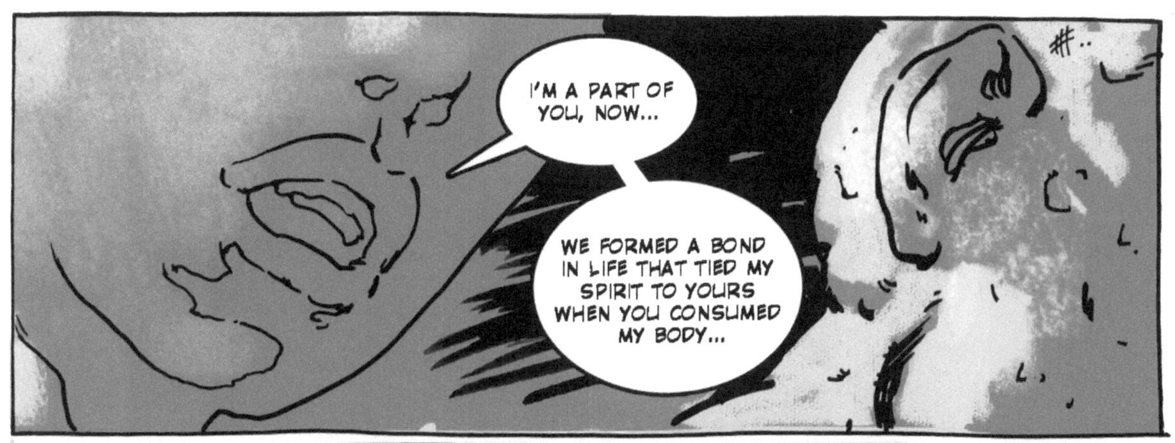

I'M A PART OF YOU, NOW...
WE FORMED A BOND IN LIFE THAT TIED MY SPIRIT TO YOURS WHEN YOU CONSUMED MY BODY...

NOW, AS YOUR STRENGTH FAILS...

...I LEND THE POWER OF MY SPIRIT TO YOURS!

KAREN?

"MY BODY AND MY SPIRIT NOW RESIDE WITHIN YOU"

ANOTHER JOURNEY LIES AHEAD FOR THIS MONSTER, EMBEDDED NOW WITH A HUMAN SPIRIT AND TEMPERED IN THE FIRES OF HEROISM.

KAREN'S WORDS STILL ECHO IN THE SMALL GHOUL'S EARS: "I DON'T KNOW IF THIS WORLD IS WORTH SAVING, ANYMORE..."
WHATEVER IS LEFT, THEY WILL TRY AND SAVE TOGETHER.

THE PAST DEMANDS A REMATCH: PASSION, PERSISTENCE & THE PULCHRITUDINOUS POWER OF PULP

CODY GOODFELLOW has written five solo novels and two more with NY times bestselling author John Skipp. Two of his collections, SILENT WEAPONS FOR QUIET WARS and ALL-MONSTER ACTION, both received the Wonderland Book Award. He wrote, co-produced and scored the short Lovecraftian hygiene film STAY AT HOME DAD, which can be viewed on YouTube. As a bishop of the Esoteric Order of Dagon he presides over several Cthulhu Prayer Breakfasts each year. He is also a co-founder of Perilous Press, an occasional micropublisher of modern cosmic horror. He currently lives in Portland, OR.

THE BROTHEL IN THE NORTH END

JEFFREY THOMAS is a prolific writer of science fiction and horror, best known for his stories set in the nightmarish future city called Punktown, such as the novel DEADSTOCK (Solaris Books) and the collection PUNK TOWN (Ministry of Whimsy Press). Other books by Thomas include the novels LETTERS FROM HADES (Bedlam Press) and MONSTROCITY (Prime Books), and the novella GODHEAD DYING DOWNWARDS (Earthling Publications). Thomas is also responsible for Necropolitan Press, an independent publisher in the genres of horror, science fiction, dark fantasy, and "the unclassifiable", which was founded in 1993 and ceased production between 2001 and March 2008.

THE CRYPT KID

MIKE DUBISCH is an internationally known fantasy illustrator and graphic novelist. His art has been used in toy design and illustration for Star Wars and Dungeons & Dragons role playing games, covers for Aliens VS Predator, the graphic adaptation of Edgar Rice Burroughs' I AM A BARBARIAN, as well as appearances in the magazines SCIENCE FICTION AGE, REALMS OF FANTASY, THE H.P. LOVECRAFT MAGAZINE of HORROR, and THE CREEPS.

DIABOLICUS INTERRUPTUS

CHRISTINE MORGAN is an active force in the Portland bizarro and weird fiction scene. She's a regular contributor to THE HORROR FICTION REVIEW. She has also edited four books into the FOSSIL LAKE anthology series. Her other interests include cheesy disaster movies, modifying Barbie dolls, and working toward becoming a crazy cat lady.

SKINNY MINNIE

JOHN SKIPP is a director, musician and New York Times best-selling horror legend. His parents almost named him Marmaduke Moses Skipp, and he's felt ripped off ever since.